JEREMIAH
LOVE & DATING
and Other Natural Disasters!

RON WHEELER

BEACON HILL PRESS OF KANSAS CITY
KANSAS CITY, MISSOURI

THE ADVENTURES OF...

JEREMIAH

by ©1988 Ron Wheeler
H-15

IT'S SPRINGTIME AGAIN AND EVERYONE'S THOUGHTS TURN TO ROMANCE.

...WELL, ALMOST EVERYONE.

OH, FRET! FRET! FRET! FRET! FRET!

WHAT'S WRONG WITH YOU, LUKE?

OH, IT'S SPRING AGAIN AND EVERYONE'S THOUGHTS TURN TO ROMANCE.

BUT MY THOUGHTS JUST TURN TO ANXIETY.

WHAT ARE YOU SO ANXIOUS ABOUT?

I'M ANXIOUS BECAUSE EVERYBODY'S GOT SOMEBODY AND I'VE GOT NOBODY.

THAT'S SILLY!

OH, FRET! FRET! FRET! FRET! FRET!

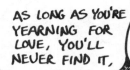

THE ADVENTURES OF... JEREMIAH

by ©1988 Ron Wheeler H-18

LUKE TRIES TO SORT OUT HIS FEELINGS FOR PAT.

I JUST HAD TO BREAK IT OFF WITH HER, JEREMIAH.

THERE WERE ALL THESE NEW AND CONFUSING FEELINGS THAT WERE HAPPENING JUST TOO FAST.

THEN I REALIZED THAT I HAD NO IDEA WHO THIS PERSON WAS THAT I WAS POURING ALL THIS EMOTION INTO.

WE NEVER EVEN GAVE OURSELVES A CHANCE TO BE FRIENDS.

IT WAS A RELATIONSHIP THAT WAS DOOMED FOR FAILURE.

BUT YOU BROKE IT OFF!

YEAH, WHEN SHE STARTED TO GET SERIOUS ABOUT ME...

...IS WHEN YOU GOT SCARED.

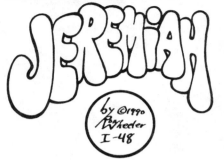

THE ADVENTURES OF...

JEREMIAH

by ©1990 Pos Wheeler I-48

LUKE, ON HIS WAY HOME FROM THE LIBRARY NOTICES SOMETHING.

GASP! A DAMSEL IN DISTRESS!

EXCUSE ME, CAN I GIVE YOU A HAND WITH THAT?

NO THANKS, I...

SAY, YOU GO TO BENTON HIGH, DON'T YOU?

SURE!

YOU DO TOO! YOU'RE AMBER CAMPBELL, SENIOR CHEERLEADER, DRAMA TEAM MEMBER, AND LEAD SINGER IN THE SCHOOL CHOIR.

I KNOW WHO YOU ARE.

MY! I'M AMAZED!

EVERYONE KNOWS WHO YOU ARE!

AND YOU ARE...

THE ADVENTURES OF...

JEREMIAH

by ©1990
Ken
Wheeler
I-49

Luke tells Jeremiah all about Amber.

SO AMBER CALLED YOU A SWEET BOY, HUH?

I'M IN LOVE, JEREMIAH.

LOVE? THAT'S NOT LOVE. THAT'S HORMONES GONE HAYWIRE!

CONTROL YOURSELF!

OH, YOU'RE JUST JEALOUS BECAUSE SHE'S NOT INTERESTED IN YOU!

AND SHE'S NOT INTERESTED IN YOU EITHER, LUKE.

SHE WAS JUST BEING NICE, SHE'S A POPULAR GIRL. POPULAR GIRLS ARE NICE TO EVERYBODY.

PLUS, SHE'S OLDER THAN YOU. SHE CALLED YOU A "BOY", REMEMBER?

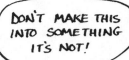

THE ADVENTURES OF...

JEREMIAH

by ©1990
Tom Wheeler
I-50

JEREMIAH FINDS LUKE WRAPPING A CHRISTMAS GIFT.

LUKE, WHAT ARE YOU DOING?

I'M GIVING AMBER A CHRISTMAS PRESENT.

A CHRISTMAS PRESENT?

YOU HARDLY KNOW THIS GIRL!

WHAT ARE YOU TALKING ABOUT? WE'RE A TIGHT COUPLE.

HAVE YOU EVEN TALKED TO HER SINCE YOU CHANGED HER TIRE?

SURE!

I SAW HER IN SCHOOL JUST THE OTHER DAY.

SHE WAS GOING DOWN THE STAIRS AND I WAS GOING UP.

THE ADVENTURES OF... JEREMIAH

by © 1990 Roy Wheeler I-52

LUKE IS DETERMINED TO ASK AMBER OUT FOR NEW YEAR'S EVE.

I TELL YA, YOU'RE SETTING YOURSELF UP FOR HEARTACHE, LUKE.

WHY DO YOU HAVE TO BE SUCH A PESSIMIST?

WHY CAN'T YOU BE ON MY SIDE?

I **AM** ON YOUR SIDE. I JUST DON'T WANT TO SEE YOU GET HURT.

YOU'RE BARKING UP THE WRONG TREE! SHE'S OUT OF YOUR LEAGUE!

OKAY! OKAY!

SNIFF! I...I...GUESS MAYBE YOU'RE RIGHT. I'M WORTHLESS!

OH, NOW I WENT AND HURT YOUR FEELINGS. YOU'RE NOT WORTHLESS, LUKE.

SNIFF

THE ADVENTURES OF...

JEREMIAH

by ©1990
Roy Wheeler
J-1

LUKE PERSISTS IN TRYING TO GET A DATE WITH AMBER CAMPBELL.

YOU CAN'T GO WITH ME TO THE SCHOOL PLAY TONIGHT, HUH?

WELL WHAT ABOUT NEXT WEEKEND? BUSY, HUH?

WELL WHAT ABOUT THE WEEKEND AFTER THAT? THE ONE AFTER THAT? AND AFTER THAT?

WOW, JEREMIAH. I DIDN'T KNOW ANYONE COULD SCHEDULE THEIR HAIR WASHING THAT FAR IN ADVANCE.

GIVE IT UP, LUKE. SHE'S OBVIOUSLY NOT INTERESTED.

BUT SHE SOUNDED SO SINCERE... LIKE SHE REALLY WANTS TO GO OUT WITH ME.

THE OLD FLATTERING REFUSALS, EH?

THE ADVENTURES OF...
JEREMIAH

by © 1990 Wheeler J-2

LUKE IS BITTER ABOUT AMBER

I DON'T KNOW HOW I COULD HAVE BEEN SO FOOLISH, JEREMIAH!

WHY DO I HAVE TO BE CLUBBED OVER THE HEAD BEFORE I WAKE UP?

AMBER CAMPBELL WASN'T INTERESTED IN ME. SHE NEVER WAS AND SHE NEVER WILL BE.

HOW COULD I BE SO BLIND?

WELCOME TO THE WACKY WORLD OF HORMONES, LUKE.

WELL THAT DOES IT! I'M NEVER TRUSTING MY FEELINGS AGAIN.

AT LEAST NOT UNTIL I PASS OUT OF PUBERTY.

DON'T BE SO HARD ON YOURSELF, LUKE.

THE ADVENTURES OF...
JEREMIAH

by ©1990 Roy Wheeler J-14

Luke tells his dating woes to his sister.

PENNY, WHY DON'T GIRLS LIKE ME?

BECAUSE YOU'RE A SLOB, I GUESS.

BUT I'M A LOVEABLE SLOB, RIGHT?

SURE, SURE, EVERY GIRL LOVES A GUY WHO CAN BELCH THE OPENING STANZA OF THE "STAR SPANGLED BANNER".

I CAN MAKE IT THROUGH THE SECOND VERSE NOW.

YIPPEE!

SURELY THERE IS SOME GIRL OUT THERE WHO WILL GO OUT WITH ME.

HOW ABOUT LUCY CRAMER?

LUCY CRAMER? WHAT ARE YOU, NUTS? SHE'S AS HOMELY AS YOU!

YOU WATCH WHAT YOU SAY, BUDDY! LUCY IS A SWEET CHRISTIAN GIRL AND A GOOD FRIEND OF MINE.

TO BE CONTINUED...

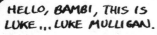

* PROV. 5:8-9

TO BE CONTINUED...

THE ADVENTURES OF... JEREMIAH

by ©1990 Roy Wheeler J-16

PENNY HEARS A VOICE COMING FROM LUKE'S ROOM.

WHAT IN THE...

OH BAMBI! YOU SHOULDN'T!

BAMBI, YOU FLATTER ME TOO MUCH. I'M NOT **THAT** WONDERFUL.

FEEL MY MUSCLES? SURE, I'LL LET YOU FEEL MY MUSCLES!

I HOPE MY EXCELLENT PHYSIQUE DOESN'T INTIMIDATE YOU TOO MUCH.

A KISS? I MUSTN'T! WELL, OKAY, JUST ONE.

SMAK

HA! HA! HA! HA! HA!

THE ADVENTURES OF... JEREMIAH

by ©1990 Joe Wheeler J-17

LUKE FINDS HIMSELF GOING OUT ON HIS DATE WITH BAMBI BIMBOWSKI AFTER ALL.

HULLO, BIG BOY!

HI, B-B-BAMBI.

COME ON IN!

GACK!

HAVE A DRINK!

A DRINK?

BEER

WHY DON'T YOU MAKE YOURSELF COMFORTABLE?

HERE! LET ME HELP.

WHAT ARE YOU DOING?

NO! NO! NO! MY BODY'S THE TEMPLE OF THE HOLY SPIRIT! YOU CAN'T HAVE IT!

TO BE CONTINUED...

THE ADVENTURES OF... JEREMIAH

by ©1980 Ray Wheeler J-24

JEREMIAH STARTS HIS NEW SUMMER JOB AT THE SUPERMARKET.

AS PART OF YOUR TRAINING THERE ARE A FEW THINGS YOU NEED TO BE AWARE OF.

FIRST OF ALL, ALWAYS BE COURTEOUS TO THE CUSTOMER. THE CUSTOMER IS ALWAYS RIGHT.

EVEN WHEN HE'S WRONG.

SECOND, YOU MUST BE NEAT IN APPEARANCE. MEN MUST WEAR TIES AND NO FACIAL HAIR.

I COULDN'T WEAR FACIAL HAIR IF I WANTED TO.

THIRD, ALWAYS RECOMMEND TO PEOPLE OUR PRIVATE LABEL BRANDS OVER THE NATIONAL BRANDS WHEN POSSIBLE.

OURS IS CHEAPER IN PRICE AND IN MANY CASES THE SAME COMPANY MAKES BOTH.

FOR EXAMPLE, OUR "SUPER SOFT" FACIAL TISSUE IS JUST AS GOOD AS THE NAME BRAND TISSUE.

SURE, IF YOU DON'T MIND BLOWING YOUR NOSE INTO SANDPAPER.

TO BE CONTINUED...

THE ADVENTURES OF...

JEREMIAH

by ©1990 Roy Wheeler J-26

JEREMIAH DEBATES WHETHER TO ASK A FELLOW SUPERMARKET EMPLOYEE OUT ON A DATE.

BOY! TINA SURE IS CUTE.

...AND FRIENDLY, TOO! SHE ALWAYS HAS A SMILE FOR ME WHEN I SACK AT HER CHECKSTAND.

I REALLY THINK I SHOULD ASK HER OUT. I'M SURE SHE WANTS TO GO OUT WITH ME.

...OR DOES SHE?

MAYBE SHE'S JUST BEING FRIENDLY.

SURELY A CUTE GIRL LIKE HER HAS A BOYFRIEND.

IF I ASK HER OUT AND SHE TURNS ME DOWN, I'LL FEEL LIKE A TOTAL IDIOT!

AND IF SHE DOES GO OUT WITH ME AND IT DOESN'T WORK OUT, HOW AM I GOING TO WORK NEXT TO HER ALL SUMMER?

TO BE CONTINUED...

THE ADVENTURES OF...

JEREMIAH

by ©1990 Wheeler
J-27

THE ADVENTURES OF...

JEREMIAH

by Wheeler ©1990
J-28

JEREMIAH AND TINA GO ON A DATE TOGETHER TO THE AMUSEMENT PARK.

WOW! LET'S RIDE THE ROLLER COASTER AGAIN.

I'M GAME IF YOU ARE.

...AND THEY HAVE AN ABSOLUTELY WONDERFUL TIME TOGETHER.

WHEEEEEEEE

EVERYTHING IS WONDERFUL ...EXCEPT, ON THE SAME EVENING, AT THE OTHER END OF THE PARK...

COME ON, TRUDY, LET'S DO ANOTHER RIDE.

NO, PENNY, I DON'T FEEL LIKE IT.

ARE YOU STILL STEWING OVER JEREMIAH?

YEAH, I KNOW IT'S SILLY, BUT HE HASN'T CALLED ME FOR A FEW DAYS.

DON'T WORRY! HE'S BEEN WORKING A LOT LATELY.

I KNOW! I KNOW! BUT SOMEHOW I FEEL LIKE THERE IS SOMETHING WRONG BETWEEN US.

HE'S SEEMED MORE DISTANT LATELY... ...LIKE THERE'S SOMETHING ELSE OCCUPYING HIS ATTENTION.

THE ADVENTURES OF... JEREMIAH

by ©1990
Tom Wheeler
J-29

MATT FINDS TRUDY CRYING HER EYES OUT.

TRUDY, WHAT'S WRONG?

OH BOO, HOO HOO!

I SAW JEREMIAH HOLDING HANDS WITH ANOTHER GIRL.

OH, I'M SO SORRY! I JUST DON'T UNDERSTAND THAT GUY.

WHAT DO YOU MEAN?

WELL I THINK HE'S REALLY CHANGED.

CHANGED?

FIRST OF ALL, HE ACED ME OUT OF A JOB THAT I TALKED HIM INTO APPLYING FOR.

I MEAN HE DELIBERATELY PUSHED HIS WAY IN AND STOLE THE JOB RIGHT OUT FROM UNDER ME.

THAT DOESN'T SOUND LIKE HIM.

TO BE CONTINUED...

THE ADVENTURES OF...

JEREMIAH

by © 1990 Ray Wheeler J-30

JEREMIAH HAS A HEART-TO-HEART TALK WITH TINA.

TINA, BEFORE WE GO ANY FURTHER IN THIS FRIENDSHIP I NEED TO KNOW ONE THING ABOUT YOU.

IF IT'S WHETHER I LIKE YOU A LOT OR NOT JEREMIAH, I **DO** LIKE YOU VERY MUCH.

WELL, I KNOW THAT... I MEAN THAT'S NOT WHAT I MEAN... ...I MEAN...

WHAT IS IT?

TINA, I LIKE YOU VERY MUCH AND I WANT TO SEE THIS RELATIONSHIP SUCCEED BUT THERE IS SOMEONE ELSE THAT IS VERY IMPORTANT IN MY LIFE.

I KNEW IT! YOU HAVE A GIRLFRIEND!

THAT'S NOT WHAT I MEAN...I MEAN I DO HAVE...OR DID HAVE... OR I DO HAVE A FRIEND THAT'S A GIRL BUT THAT'S NOT WHAT I'M TALKING ABOUT.

I'M CONFUSED.

TINA, DO YOU KNOW ANYTHING ABOUT CHRISTIANITY?

YOU MEAN RIGHT-WING FUNDAMENTALIST BIGOTRY?

I GUESS THAT SORT OF ANSWERS MY QUESTION.

YOU'RE NOT SOME RELIGIOUS QUACK, ARE YOU?

THE ADVENTURES OF...

by Wheeler
J-31

JEREMIAH TALKS TO TRUDY LIKE A WHIPPED PUPPY.

I'M REALLY SORRY ABOUT HOW ALL THIS HAS WORKED OUT, TRUDY.

THAT'S OKAY, JEREMIAH. I HAVE NO CLAIM ON YOU.

YEAH, WELL I THINK I PROBABLY COULD HAVE COMMUNICATED WITH YOU A LITTLE BETTER.

SO WHERE IS TINA?

SHE'S STILL WORKING AT THE SUPERMARKET. IT BECAME OBVIOUS THAT SHE HAD ABSOLUTELY NO INTEREST IN BECOMING A CHRISTIAN.

WHAT'S AMAZING IS THAT APART FROM THAT SHE IS SO NORMAL.

...AND SHE'S AMAZED THAT I'M SO NORMAL FOR BEING A CHRISTIAN.

TO ME, THE FACT THAT TWO NORMAL PEOPLE CAN LOOK AT THE SAME EVIDENCE AND DRAW COMPLETELY OPPOSITE CONCLUSIONS...

THE ADVENTURES OF... JEREMIAH

by ©1989 Wheeler I-15

LUKE SPOTS AN OLD FRIEND

UH-OH, JEREMIAH, DON'T LOOK NOW.

WHAT IS IT?

DO YOU REMEMBER THAT GIRL I WENT OUT WITH A YEAR AGO?

YOU WENT OUT WITH A GIRL?

COME ON, JEREMIAH.

OH, YES, I REMEMBER, SHE SORT OF LIKED YOU, DIDN'T SHE?

SORT OF LIKED ME? SHE WAS HEAD-OVER-HEELS MADLY IN LOVE WITH ME!

YEAH, SHE MUST HAVE REALLY BEEN WARPED.

I BEG YOUR PARDON.

I'LL HAVE YOU KNOW THAT I'M A PRIME CATCH FOR SOME LUCKY GIRL.

SURE! SURE!

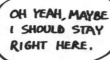

THE ADVENTURES OF... JEREMIAH

by ©1989 Ralheeler I-16

LUKE VISITS WITH AN OLD FLAME.

LUKE, YOU REALLY HURT ME WHEN YOU STOPPED DATING ME A YEAR AGO.

I KNOW.

I FELT LIKE I REALLY MADE MYSELF VULNERABLE TO YOU...

I KNOW.

...AND YOU JUST STEPPED ON MY FEELINGS.

I KNOW.

AND IT WAS THE BEST LESSON I EVER LEARNED.

HUH?

I LEARNED THAT I DON'T NEED TO RUSH LOVE BY THROWING MYSELF AT SOMEONE...

REALLY!

...BUT THAT I SHOULD JUST BE MYSELF, TRUST IN THE LORD, AND LET FRIENDSHIPS WITH THE OPPOSITE SEX DEVELOP AT A NATURAL PACE.

THAT'S GREAT!

THE ADVENTURES OF... JEREMIAH

by ©1989 Jay/Wheeler I-17

JEREMIAH CONSOLES LUKE.

WHAT ARE YOU SO UPSET ABOUT, LUKE?

PAT WON'T GO OUT WITH ME

SO WHAT? YOU NEVER WANTED TO GO OUT WITH HER FOR THE LAST YEAR, WHY DO YOU WANT TO GO OUT WITH HER NOW?

BECAUSE SHE'S DATING THE CAPTAIN OF THE FOOTBALL TEAM.

SO?

SHE'S HIGHER THAN ME ON THE "COOL" SCALE NOW

HUH?

BEFORE, WHEN SHE WANTED ME MORE THAN I WANTED HER, SHE WAS LOWER THAN ME ON THE "COOL" SCALE.

NOW, BY DATING THE TOP HUNK IN SCHOOL, THAT PUTS HER AT THE TOP OF THE CHART.

TO BE CONTINUED...

THE ADVENTURES OF...

JEREMIAH

by ©1981 Roy Wheeler I-18

LUKE PICKS UP PAT TO GO ON A DATE...

HI, PAT, READY TO GO?

...ALONG WITH HER BOYFRIEND, BRUNO.

GRUNT!

COME ON, BRUNO. LUKE'S WAITING.

THIS IS SO STRANGE! HOW DID I LET MYSELF GET INTO THIS TYPE OF SITUATION?

I'VE GOT TO THINK OF SOME WAY TO GET RID OF THIS BRUNO CHARACTER!

I KNOW! I'LL INTRODUCE HIM TO MY SISTER, PENNY.

LET'S GO TO BURGER DOODLES.

SOUNDS GOOD TO ME.

GRUNT!

* TRANSLATION: DO YOU HAVE A BOYFRIEND OR ARE YOU GOING TO STEAL BRUNO?

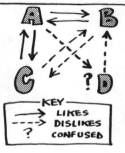

THE ADVENTURES OF...
JEREMIAH

by ©1989
Wheeler
I-20

MATT IS ABOUT TO GET POUNDED.

WHAT YOU CALL ME?

GACK!

BRUNO, PUT HIM DOWN!

HUH?

I SAID, PUT HIM DOWN! NOW!

DUH! OKAY!

THUD!

NOW, SAY YOU'RE SORRY.

I SORRY!

AHEM... CHOKE... IT'S OKAY. I'LL BE ABLE TO SWALLOW IN A WEEK OR SO.

I'M ASHAMED OF YOU.

I SORRY!

COME ALONG NOW. I'M TAKING YOU HOME!

I SORRY!

THE ADVENTURES OF...

JEREMIAH

by ©1991 Roy Wheeler
K-15

THE BIG SCHOOL PARTY IS COMING

BIG PARTY
BENTON HIGH

EXCUSE ME?

SO, TRUDY, WHAT ARE YOU GOING TO WEAR TO THE PARTY SATURDAY?

SHOULD WE GO DRESSED UP OR CASUAL?

YOU'RE FORGETTING ONE THING.

WHAT'S THAT?

YOU HAVEN'T ASKED ME TO GO YET.

OH, I'M SORRY, TRUDY, WOULD YOU LIKE TO GO TO THE SCHOOL PARTY WITH ME SATURDAY NIGHT?

I'M NOT SURE.

YOU'RE NOT SURE? OH, COME ON, TRUDY.

LOOK! NOBODY LIKES BEING TAKEN FOR GRANTED.

QUIT BEING SILLY!

SILLY?

THE ADVENTURES OF...

JEREMIAH

by ©1991
Tony Wheeler
K-16

TRUDY AND JEREMIAH ARE ON THE SKIDS.

JEREMIAH, I WOULD NEVER GO OUT WITH YOU AGAIN IF YOU WERE THE LAST MAN ON EARTH!

DOES THIS MEAN WE HAVE NO DATE FOR THE PARTY SATURDAY?

IT MEANS I NEVER WANT TO SEE YOU AGAIN!

JUST WHAT ARE YOU TRYING TO SAY?

AAAAUUGH!

HOW CAN I GET THROUGH YOUR THICK SKULL?

IS THERE SOMEONE ELSE?

NO! NO! NO! THERE'S...

WAIT A MINUTE... YES, THERE IS SOMEONE ELSE.

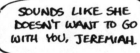

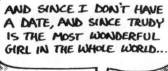

TO BE CONTINUED...

THE ADVENTURES OF...

JEREMIAH

by ©1991
Ron
Wheeler
K-17

TRUDY HAS BROKEN UP WITH JEREMIAH AND IS NOW GOING WITH LUKE TO THE BIG SCHOOL PARTY.

WELL, IF THAT'S THE WAY SHE WANTS IT, TWO CAN PLAY THIS GAME.

SAY, JANICE, WOULD YOU LIKE TO GO TO THE SCHOOL PARTY WITH ME SATURDAY NIGHT?

SORRY, JEREMIAH. I ALREADY HAVE A DATE.

ALLISON, CAN YOU GO WITH ME TO THE PARTY SATURDAY?

ASKING KIND OF LATE, AREN'T YOU, JEREMIAH?

NO THANKS!

HOW ABOUT YOU, JENNY?

FORGET IT!

LINDA, YOU'RE MY LAST HOPE. I'M LOOKING FOR SOMEONE TO GO TO THE SCHOOL PARTY WITH ME SATURDAY NIGHT.

I KNOW.

THE ADVENTURES OF... JEREMIAH

by ©1991 Ron Wheeler
K-18

TO BE CONTINUED...

THE ADVENTURES OF...

JEREMIAH

by ©1991
Ron Wheeler
K-20

JEREMIAH LEVELS WITH GLORIA.

GLORIA, I HAVE TO LEVEL WITH YOU.

LEVEL WITH ME?

YOU HATE ME, DON'T YOU? I KNEW IT! I KNEW IT!

NO, I DON'T HATE YOU.

YOU LOVE ME?

NO, I DON'T LOVE YOU, I LIKE YOU.

LIKE ME?

LIKE ME AS IN SOME DAY YOU COULD LOVE ME?

OR LIKE ME AS YOU WOULD LIKE ICE CREAM.

THE ADVENTURES OF...

JEREMIAH

by ©1991
Roy Wheeler
K-21

TRUDY AND LUKE ARE HAVING A LOUSY TIME AT THE BIG SCHOOL PARTY.

CAN I GET YOU SOME MORE PUNCH, TRUDY?

NO THANKS, LUKE.

YOU DON'T WANT TO BE HERE WITH ME, DO YOU?

NO, NO, I'M HAVING FUN, AREN'T YOU?

IT'S OKAY, TRUDY, I UNDERSTAND. YOUR MIND IS SOMEWHERE ELSE.

YOU WISH YOU WERE WITH JEREMIAH, DON'T YOU?

WELL, I WISH I HADN'T BLOWN UP AT HIM.

WELL, HERE'S YOUR CHANCE TO MAKE YOUR APOLOGY. HE JUST ARRIVED.

HI, GUYS. TRUDY AND LUKE, THIS IS GLORIA.

THE ADVENTURES OF...

JEREMIAH

by ©1991
Ray Wheeler
K-37

TRUDY HAS SOME BIG NEWS FOR JEREMIAH.

YOU'RE WHAT?

I SAID MY PARENTS ARE TAKING ME OUT OF TOWN WITH THEM FOR MOST OF THIS FALL.

BUT THAT'S A LONG TIME!

I THOUGHT YOU'D BE EXCITED FOR ME.

I AM, BUT...

I'LL GET TO SEE PLACES I'VE NEVER SEEN BEFORE.

...AND I'VE GOT ALL MY HOMEWORK ASSIGNMENTS SO I WON'T GET BEHIND, AND IT'S A GOLDEN OPPORTUNITY, AND...

...AND I'LL MISS YOU.

THE ADVENTURES OF... JEREMIAH

by ©1991 Ray Wheeler K-39

PENNY'S IN A DAZE BECAUSE SHE THINKS JEREMIAH "LOVES" HER.

HMMM. HE SAID HE'S SEEN LOTS AND LOTS OF GIRLS WHO ARE FAR FAR UGLIER THAN ME.

YEP! HE... HE...LOVES ME.

PENNY! WATCH OUT!

HONK! HONK! HONK!

SCREECH

PUSH

ZOOOM!

CRASH

JEREMIAH, ARE YOU ALL RIGHT?

GROAN!

OH, JEREMIAH! JEREMIAH! YOU SAVED MY LIFE! ARE YOU OKAY?

THE ADVENTURES OF... JEREMIAH

by ©1991 Tony Wheeler
K-40

JEREMIAH INJURES HIMSELF SAVING PENNY'S LIFE.

OH HI, PENNY.

YOU TAKING VISITORS, JEREMIAH?

KNOCK KNOCK

I'M GLAD YOU CAME BY. I THINK WE NEED TO TALK.

YEAH, I KNOW.

LOOK, JEREMIAH, I HOPE YOU DON'T THINK I'M SOME SORT OF AN IDIOT FOR SPILLING MY GUTS TO YOU LIKE I DID.

NO! NO!

I MEAN, I WISH I HADN'T SAID ALL THOSE THINGS. I WISH I COULD TAKE BACK THE WORDS.

BUT ON THE OTHER HAND, I'M GLAD YOU FINALLY KNOW HOW I FEEL ABOUT YOU. I DON'T HAVE TO HOLD IT IN ANY LONGER.

I DIDN'T WANT TO FALL IN LOVE WITH YOU, JEREMIAH. IT'S JUST THAT YOU'RE SO NICE AND YOU'RE SO COMMITTED TO SERVING CHRIST.

THE ADVENTURES OF...

JEREMIAH

by ©1991
Ron Wheeler
K-42

TRUDY COMES BACK FROM A FAMILY TRIP.

HI, PENNY.

OH, HI, TRUDY.

GASP! MY RIVAL!

HOW CAN I FACE MY BEST FRIEND WHEN I JUST TOLD HER BOYFRIEND THAT I LOVE HIM.

WELL, AREN'T YOU GOING TO INVITE ME IN?

S...SURE! SURE! COME IN!

ANYTHING HAPPEN WHILE I WAS GONE?

UH...NOT MUCH.

YEAH, RIGHT!

WHAT AM I SUPPOSED TO SAY?

I MADE A PLAY FOR YOUR BOYFRIEND WHILE YOU WERE GONE, TRUDY?

WAIT A MINUTE! MAYBE SHE ALREADY KNOWS!

MAYBE JEREMIAH ALREADY TOLD HER AND SHE'S WAITING TO SEE IF I'LL COME FOREWARD AND BE HONEST WITH HER.

MAYBE I **SHOULD** TELL HER.

NO, IT WOULD ONLY HURT HER FEELINGS. NOTHING GOOD WOULD COME OF IT AND I WOULD LOSE MY BEST FRIEND.

LORD, WHAT DO YOU WANT ME TO DO?

SO HAVE YOU SEEN JEREMIAH SINCE YOU'VE BEEN BACK?

YEAH, I JUST CAME FROM THERE.

GULP! YOU DID?

BOY, HE TOOK A NASTY **FALL** AND GOT A **LOVELY** ANKLE SPRAIN. IT'S REALLY **CRUSHED.**

FALL? LOVE? CRUSH? **YOU KNOW!**

OH TRUDY, I WASN'T PLANNING TO **FALL** IN **LOVE** AND HAVE A **CRUSH** ON JEREMIAH.

HUH?

TO BE CONTINUED...

THE ADVENTURES OF... JEREMIAH

by ©1991
Ron Wheeler
K-43

PENNY COMES CLEAN AND TELLS TRUDY OF HER CRUSH ON JEREMIAH.

HUH?

I WASN'T PLANNING TO FALL IN LOVE WITH JEREMIAH. IT JUST HAPPENED.

WHAT ARE YOU TALKING ABOUT?

OH, STOP PRETENDING, TRUDY.

JEREMIAH TOLD YOU OF THE TIME WE SPENT TOGETHER WHILE YOU WERE GONE, DIDN'T HE?

WHAT?

HE WAS SO NICE AND CONSIDERATE. I COULDN'T HELP FALLING IN LOVE.

WHAT?

YOU MEAN HE DIDN'T TELL YOU ABOUT ...US?

THAT TWO TIMER!

OH, I'M SORRY. I HOPE THIS DOESN'T AFFECT OUR FRIENDSHIP.

I'M GOING TO GIVE HIM A PIECE OF MY MIND.

TO BE CONTINUED...

THE ADVENTURES OF...

by ©1991 Ron Wheeler K-44

OUR FRIENDS DISCUSS WHAT TO DO ABOUT PENNY'S CRUSH ON JEREMIAH.

WHAT SHOULD I DO? HURT HER FEELINGS SO SHE WON'T HAVE A CRUSH ON ME ANY MORE?

NO, YOU CAN'T DO THAT.

SHE KNOWS YOU TOO WELL. SHE'LL SEE THRU THAT.

BESIDES, YOU COULDN'T HURT SOMEONE'S FEELINGS INTENTIONALLY IF YOU TRIED.

YEAH, I GUESS YOU'RE RIGHT.

YOU KNOW, I CAN'T HELP BUT FEEL LIKE THESE KINDS OF CRUSHES ARE NOT OF GOD.

YOU CAN SAY THAT AGAIN.

I THINK WHEN SOMEONE IS INFATUATED LIKE THAT THEY MUST BE LOOKING FOR THAT PERSON TO FILL A VOID THAT ONLY THE LORD CAN FILL.

MAYBE WE SHOULD PRAY THAT PENNY WOULD TRUST THE LORD SO MUCH THAT HE WOULD MAKE HER FEEL SECURE ENOUGH SHE WOULDN'T HAVE CRUSHES.

THE ADVENTURES OF...

JEREMIAH

by ©1992
Tom Wheeler
L-30

PENNY AND LUKE BATTLE OVER LUKE'S EATING HABITS.

HEY! GIMME BACK THOSE TWINKIES!

I'M SAVING YOU FROM YOURSELF!

BUT WHO'S GOING TO SAVE YOU FROM ME?

GACK!

OKAY! OKAY! EAT THIS JUNK! SEE WHAT I CARE!

WOP!

MMMMM!

THAT STUFF'S POISON I TELL YOU.

IT'S SO FULL OF CHOLESTEROL YOUR ARTERIES ARE GOING INTO RIGOR MORTIS.

OOOO! WHAT'S THAT SOUND?

THE ADVENTURES OF...
JEREMIAH

by ©1992 Ron Wheeler
L-31

LUKE GETS ON A FITNESS KICK!

16-17-18-19-20!

WOW, LUKE! YOU'RE REALLY GETTING INTO SHAPE!

YEAH, AND I FEEL GOOD TOO!

I DON'T KNOW WHY I DIDN'T THINK OF DOING THIS SOONER.

PENNY, WHY DIDN'T YOU TELL ME TO WATCH WHAT I EAT AND GET IN SHAPE?

OH BROTHER!

YOU MUST BE PROUD OF YOUR BROTHER, PENNY.

I DON'T KNOW...

IT'S GOOD THAT HE'S WORKING OUT AND EATING RIGHT...

THE ADVENTURES OF...

JEREMIAH

by ©1992
Tom Wheeler
L-32

THE ADVENTURES OF...

JEREMIAH

by ©1992
Roy Wheeler
L-33

WITH HIS NEW "LOOK", LUKE STARTS DATING LOTS OF GIRLS.

SOMETIMES HE HAD A DIFFERENT GIRL ON HIS ARM EVERY WEEK.

SOMETIMES HE HAD SEVERAL GIRLS AROUND HIM AT THE SAME TIME.

GO EASY ON ME, GIRLS. I'M FRAGILE.

BOY, JEREMIAH, THIS IS REALLY WILD!

YOU'RE PRETTY HAPPY HUH?

I'M GOING OUT WITH A DIFFERENT GIRL EVERY NIGHT AND THREE DATES ON THE WEEKENDS.

SO ARE YOU HAPPY?

MY SOCIAL LIFE HAS GONE FROM NERD TO DATE KING OVERNIGHT SINCE I CHANGED MY IMAGE.

BUT ARE YOU HAPPY?

POPULAR, BEAUTIFUL GIRLS ARE NOW CLAMORING TO GO OUT WITH ME.

SO I GUESS YOU'RE PRETTY MISERABLE, HUH?